Richard of Conisbrough

A play in the style of William Shakespeare

CHRISTOPHER WEBSTER

DEDICATION

To my Advanced English class with whom I am studying *Richard III* to which this play is a sort of prequel.

CONTENTS

O for a Muse of fire, that would ascend
The brightest heaven of invention,
A kingdom for a stage, princes to act
And monarchs to behold the swelling scene!
Then should the warlike Harry, like himself,
Assume the port of Mars; and at his heels,
Leashed in like hounds, should famine, sword and fire
Crouch for employment. But pardon, and gentles all,
The flat unraised spirits that have dared
On this unworthy scaffold to bring forth
So great an object.

—HENRY V, William Shakespeare

INTRODUCTION

Thirty years ago I went to watch a performance of a Shakespeare play at Sheffield Playhouse. I was horrified when the characters walked onto the stage wearing modern suits. It turned out that I had come on the wrong night and that the play was actually *The Importance of Being Ernest*. Nevertheless, I have seen Shakespeare plays acted in all manner of inappropriate costume, and it is a fashion which still blights the stage today.

If this play is ever performed, I hope that the costumes will at least approximate to those of early fifteenth century England. The scenery can be minimal. A backdrop depicting a stone wall with a hint of castle about it (for example, a parapet), an arched window and a door should do it. The door is important because Peter is often hovering on one side of a door or another.

My ideal performance would take place in the Conisbrough Castle bailey in the *son et lumière* style. Rows of temporary seating would be set up facing the keep, and a small stage erected at the bottom of it. The keep steps, the upper windows, the top of the keep, and parts of the wall walk (if allowed by Health and Safety busybodies) could be used for parts of the performance, each area picked out by spotlights as appropriate.

The play is part of my series about the history of Conisbrough Castle, which includes Crusader, Allan-a-Dale and Adela, The Squire and the Lady, The Poet and the Castle, and concludes with Conisbrough Castle, a history of the castle from an author's perspective.

The story of Richard of Conisbrough is well suited to a play in the style of William Shakespeare. Part of the subject matter, the Southampton Plot, was treated by the bard in his play *Henry V*, and the main character is typical of many 'bastard' malcontents of Elizabethan drama, such as Don John in Measure for Measure.

Another reason for choosing the form was that I was teaching Richard III to an Advanced Literature class, and in an unguarded moment, boasted that I could write a similar play. Well, this is it. If there are any similarities, it is because I 'borrowed' a few lines (OK, more than a few) from my favourite Shakespeare plays.

As it happens, the story of Richard of Conisbrough is a kind of prequel to the story of Richard III, because he is a direct descendant through his son, Richard of York.

I enjoyed writing it, though it is unlikely ever to be performed. Perhaps if I were a teacher at the De Warenne Academy in Conisbrough, I could make it happen, but as the school where I am teaching at present is 6,740 miles away, that is unlikely.

However, if my dream performance in the bailey of the castle is ever staged, don't forget to invite me!

Christopher Webster, July 2016/2024

DRAMATIS PERSONAE

PETER – a page, who also acts as the chorus (a fictional character).

CONISBROUGH/CAMBRIDGE – Richard of Conisbrough, later the Earl of Cambridge.

SERJEANT GOODLAD – Serjeant-at-arms of Conisbrough Castle (a fictional character).

TOM, DICK AND HARRY – men-at-arms of Conisbrough Castle (fictional characters).

KING HENRY IV – King of England from 1399 to 1413.

LADY ELEANOR – Eleanor Holland, Countess of March (1370 – 1405).

ANNE – Anne de Mortimer, Countess of Cambridge (1390 – 1411).

MEG – a kitchen maid at Hereford Castle (a fictional character).

FITZ HUGH – Henry FitzHugh, Bishop of Bath.

GREY – Sir Thomas Grey (1384 – 1415), of Castle Heaton near Norham.

SCROPE – Henry Scrope, 3rd Baron Scrope of Masham KG (c.1370 – 1415).

HANS and LEIF – Danish men-at-arms (fictional characters).

GREY – Sir Thomas Grey of Heaton in Norham, Northumberland.

LEECH – a doctor (a fictional character).

PRIEST (a fictional character).

KING HENRY V – King of England from 1413 to 1422.

EXETER – John St. Holland, 1st Duke of Exeter.

ACT I

Enter PETER. He is carrying a tankard of ale to his lord who is waiting impatiently in the Great Chamber of the keep. At first he is unaware of the audience, but noticing them, he addresses them directly.

PETER

Who's that? Oh, ah know. Tha's come to watch Webster's play. Well, I should warn thee that Webster is not t' Swan o' Avon. Far from it – the Crow o' Conisbrough more like! But who else is there to tell t' tale? The bard himself gid us a bit on it in *Henry V*, but usually our great writers dunna bother themselves about a rough 'n ready place like Conisbrough. Anyway, Webster did his best. He wrote a lot o' t' lines in iambic pentameters – remember 'em from the De Warenne Acadamy? No? Well, ne' mind, hey? 'Ee did some other fancy stuff an' all: 'ee made one of the speeches into a sonnet – imagine that! – an 'ee a Conisbrough lad! Another thing – 'ee gid it fair few 'thees' an' 'thous' – but I dunna 'ave to explain that to thee 'cos that's 'ow you lot speak – when you're not tryin' to be posh, that is! What ah'm trying to say is that, though Webster did 'is best, 'ee's no Shakespeare – and that's weer ah come in. Ah'll help thee to get through t' next five hours – only kiddin', it's not that long, even though it might feel like it – by explaining things from time to time. But ah can't linger nah 'cos ah've got to tek this tankard to me lordship who's a bit t' worse for wear after a neet on t' parapet, as we say in fourteenth century England.

Oh, ah forgot. This is Conisbrough Castle – but yer know that already. Me master is Richard o' Conisbrough, and t' year is 1399.

SCENE 1

The guard room on the ground floor of the keep. Men-at-arms, TOM, DICK and HARRY are awaiting orders from SERJEANT GOODLAD. PETER enters with the tankard of ale and hurries past the men-at-arms. We hear CONISBROUGH'S voice echoing from the Great Chamber above.

CONISBROUGH
Page! Page! Where is the boy?

PETER

                              Coming, my lord!

CONISBROUGH
Then hurry up! Have I to wait all day?
to taste a little of the dog that bit me
and drive away the devils in my head?

There is more of the same until PETER reappears in the guardroom rubbing his head as though he has just received a blow.

SERGEANT
How is my lord of Conisbrough this morning?

PETER

'Ee's in a mood as black as – well, a black dog – for
when he's drained t' ale butt dahn to't bottom 'ee's like
to bark, an' what's worse, to bite! Well, no, he didna bite
– just clipped me rahnd t' ear oil!

SERJEANT GOODLAD
Well then, I'll go up later to receive my orders
and place the sentries as I placed them yesterday.

To three men-at-arms waiting nearby.

You, Tom, it's your turn to do gatehouse duty.
You, Harry, man the walk around the walls.
You, Dick, go to the keep. The very top.

DICK
But, sarge! my lord is in one o' his rages, an' ah must go
reet past 'is chamber when ah gus up t' stairs to t' turret.

TOM
What put 'im out o' sorts?

SERJEANT GOODLAD
Methinks it must have been that messenger,
who came last night with letters from King Henry.
Ill news, perhaps, though for a while he seemed
merry enough, carousing, calling out,
"What care I for King Henry, am I not
Richard of Conisbrough, of noble birth,
son of a Duke – although not sure which one!"

DICK
I 'eard it too, for I was on guard outside t'hall. I thought
at first 'ee said the words wi' pride, but fer them last
words an' that strange laugh he ended wi'. It sounded as
'ollow as t' inside of me belly feels nah, wi' still an 'our

to breakfast!
SERJEANT GOODLAD
Well, go. But, mark my words, go quietly.
Take off those steely sabatons – not yet!
Thy feet stink worse than fish! But take them off
inside the keep and creep up to the turret
as lightly as a fairy on her toes.

HARRY
Aye, that's the word! That's what 'ee is inside that suit
of armour! A gret big fairy!

SERGEANT
Are you still here? By now you should be thrice
around the circuit of the inner bailey.
If you don't get yourself out of my sight
you'll be up there until tomorrow night!

Exeunt omnes.

SCENE 2

*The Great Chamber in the keep. CONISBROUGH is
pacing up and down, while PETER waits for orders.*

CONISBROUGH
Ah happy days! Ah happy, happy days!
Childhood. Which to mankind is like an Eden
before the tasting of the poison fruit
of Good and Evil. How I loved to play
within these weathered walls! With wooden sword
and basin from the kitchens for a helm
I was a knight! The best of knights, no less.
King Arthur, and a battered plank of wood
was the Round Table. Or, in the Castle Woods,
bending a bow made from a willow branch,

I was bold Robin Hood, and made the servants
take on the role of Robin's enemies.
That steep escarpment, terror to our foes,
was but a place to play at roly-poly,
and if my father frowned at my mad frolics
I laughed at him and hid under the drawbridge.
When did they pass, those days, those happy days,
when life was merrier than a skylark's song,
when I could be whoever I wished to be
with no bound – only my imagination?
When did I learn I was that hated creature
that men call bastard? That my father
was not my father, though he said he loved me,
and that the man who really was my father
was his wife's lover. What was I, then?
A token of her infidelity
that he could not escape and could not love?
And yet he said he loved me, though he left
me nothing in his will. And now the king
dares to revoke the miserly allowance
that my poor mother won by intercession
from good King Richard. Yet I'll show them all!
I'll rise above my birth, bastard or not,
and show them what this Conisbrough boy is made of!

PETER *(aside)*

'Ee's not the only one wi' 'appy childhood memories. Ah've a few – though not many, 'cos ah've been working as long as ah can remember. It was when ah were ten, ah think. Ah were playing ball wi' Moll t' kitchen maid, an' Dirk t' Farrier's lad just in front o' t' keep. Moll threw t' ball reet o'er Dirk's 'ead an' it landed somewheer in t' corner between t' keep and t' curtain wall. "Ah'll find it," she said. Dirk went after her, but she said, "No, not thee, Peter." So ah followed 'er, an' when we were aht o' sight behind the buttress, she kissed me. "What were that fer?" I said. "Love," she said. Then Sergeant Goodlad caught us playin' an' sent us back to work – I'll bet my lord o' Conisbrough never had his childhood games interrupted like that!

Peter looks round as he hears footsteps passing outside. The footsteps are all the more suspicious because of their attempt to be unheard.

CONISBROUGH
But hark, what is that sound? Come here, Sirrah!
How dare you spy upon me!"

Enter DICK.

DICK

          Please, me lord,
Ah was but goin' to t' place assigned
by Sergeant Goodlad – the top o' t' keep.

CONISBOUGH
I'll have your head for this, for you have heard
every word I said about King Henry.
Why, 'tis like you will proclaim me as a traitor!

DICK
Not I, me lord. Ah'm just a man-at-arms,
and never think o' things above me station.

CONISBOUGH
Then get thee gone! But mark, I will remember,
and one more error sends thee to the dungeon.
You know the dungeon here?

DICK

          Ah do, me lord.

'Tis dug so deep ah'd fear meself in Hell.
CONISBOUGH
Then think on't and be good, and now begone!

Exit DICK.

That dungeon is not deeper than this pit:
in which the king has flung me – a nobleman
without a penny to his name this morning!
Why, the humblest cottager in Conisbrough
has more than I. He owns his humble hovel
and has, perhaps, a pig in his backyard
a cow upon the Common – and his pride.
Better by far to be a prisoner
under that vaulted roof below this keep
where there's no window and the only door
is a locked iron grate high in the ceiling.
I'd find a way to climb that wall somehow,
though it be inward sloping, and get out!
In the same way I'll climb out of this pit,
and keep on climbing till I reach the top,
and only when I've got there will I stop!

PETER *(aside)*
So that's what's eating 'im. No money! 'Ee should see t'
inside of my pocket! Shall ah tell yer what's theer? A
'ole!

ACT II

PROLOGUE

Enter PETER.

PETER
They say that every man gets 'is chance, an' a few years later, in 1403, it looked as though me lord o' Conisbrough got 'is. The king – that's good King Henry IV – sent for 'im to help 'im fight against Owain Glyndŵr on t' Welsh border. So in this scene yer must imagine that these are t' walls o' Hereford Castle. Just think double, no – mek that triple – for ah soon found art that Hereford Castle is a darned sight bigger than Conisbrough!

SCENE 1

The Great Hall at Hereford Castle. KING HENRY IV is sitting in state at one end of the hall while CONISBROUGH kneels before him. PETER and several other knights wait to one side.

KING HENRY IV
Did I not make him my Royal Lieutenant
to fight against that rebel, Owain Glyndŵr?
But often, when a man is raised too high,
he scorns the hand that helped him. So with him,
Sir Henry Percy. Yet he served me well
against my enemies, the Scots and French,

a very lion on the battlefield,
hence his cognomen, Hotspur. He would spur
his horse into the fray when others fled;
hotblooded Harry would lead men from the front
Ah Harry Hotspur, would you had stayed loyal!
But when you treated with mine enemy,
Owain Glyndŵr, and made a pact with him,
I had no choice, but had to bring you down,
slew you at Shrewsbury, gave you a traitor's end:
quartered your body, and then, ha, ha, and then
I set you up again – at least set up your head
at Micklegate, displayed upon the bar
as a dire warning to those who plot treachery!
Well, he is history, Conisbrough, and now you
must fill his place – no, not as Royal Lieutenant,
but in a lesser role where you must prove yourself
as guardian of this marcher state and castle.

CONISBROUGH
My liege, it is my honour to obey.

KING HENRY IV
What force have you to garrison this city?

CONISBOUGH
Alas, my liege, I have but twenty men.

KING HENRY IV
What, only twenty for a town this size?

CONISBOUGH *(aside)*
Aye, what am I to do with empty coffers?
If he had honoured my annuities
I might have brought an army worth the name.
Dare I beseech him now? The time's not right.
Nor is it right that I should treat in person.

I'll let it pass for now.

(To the king)
                              The garrison
is more than thirty men.

KING HENRY IV
                              And I will give
another fifty – and that must suffice.
The walls are strong, Glyndŵr will not lay siege,
without siege engines, but will hit and run –
but mark my words, Herefordshire is safe
while Hereford Castle stands. On no account
must you neglect defence to fight the enemy.

CONISBOUGH
A thousand Sirens could not tempt me hence
when good King Henry bids me man the walls.

(Aside)
This is my chance to rise! Should grim Glyndŵr
invest this castle with his mightiest force
and I hold out, and even drive him back,
perhaps the king will recognise my valour,
make me a knight, give me a grant of land,
and put my lost annuities in my hand.

Exit CONISBROUGH

SCENE 2

*The bower in Hereford Castle keep. LADY ELEANOR,
her daughter, ANNE, and Anne's DUENNA are talking
to CONISBROUGH. PETER is in attendance.*

LADY ELEANOR

This tapestry is tiring to my fingers.

ANNE
The subject is more tiring – hunting scenes
are not much to my taste.

LADY ELEANOR

What would you have?

ANNE
A scene from old romance: Arthur and Guinevere,
Lancelot of the Lake, the Holy Grail.
What do you like, duenna?

DUENNA

What is that?
Oh, yes, the tapestry. Mine eyes are dim
and I am only fit to hem the edges.

LADY ELEANOR
While we are working we must stitch my wimple.
The trimming's coming loose. I'll go and get it.

CONISBOUGH
Alone at last! I thought I'd die of boredom!

ANNE
We're not alone. There's my duenna there,
and your page Peter – I'd call it a crowd.

CONISBOUGH
A deaf old woman! She'll not bother us,
and Peter never, ever tells a secret.
So I can tell you what is in my heart.

ANNE

Your heart, my lord? What's that to do with me?

CONISBROUGH
Pray, listen to my plaint, and you will see.

He fumbles to get out a paper and reads:

Shall I compare thee to an April shower?
You were as sudden and just as reviving
And now without your presence every hour
I ask myself, how can I go on living?

An April shower nourishes green shoots
and in my heart a new love blossomed forth
and now it has wide branches and deep roots
in short, it is a love of mighty worth.

An April shower swills away the dross
of Winter's deaths of leaf and fruit and flower
And you console me, though I've suffered loss
That's why I want your presence every hour.

The showers of April lead to Summer sun
If you'll be mine, my Summer has begun!

PETER *(aside)*
An execrable sonnet, an' yer should've heard t' first
version! The next to last line was:

If you'll be mine, April will turn to summer

Which i'n't bad, but yer should've seen 'ow 'ee
struggled to think o' a rhyme for 'summer'. Ah almost
suggested one:

But if you won't – my life will be a bummer!

Well, 'ee got there in t' end, and Anne seems pleased
enough, though she's doing 'er best to 'ide it.

ANNE
But I am much too young to think of love,
I'm not fourteen.

CONISBOUGH
                        Neither was Juliet
in the old story, but it didn't stop her.
Many a woman's married at your age –
with children, too! There's no need to be shy!
I am no Romeo, perhaps, but look –
my face, I think, cannot be called unpleasing
I have a well turned leg and no pot belly.
Perhaps my poverty makes you pretend
that you're too young to love. Perhaps my birth –
my bastardy (vile word!) – has put you off.
But I will rise above my blighted birth
and win such honours as will make us rich.

ANNE
In truth, good sir, I am more than a child
and would much rather have a man to hold
than my poor wooden doll. I like you well,
but feared to seem too forward in my answer.

CONISBOUGH
These words are sweet! So marry me at once!

ANNE
It is an honour that I dream not of.

CONISBOUGH
Well, think of marriage now. Younger than you
Here in Conisbrough, ladies of esteem

Are made already mothers, as I said.

ANNE
Good sir, how can I? I am never free.
My mother watches me and my duenna.

CONISBOUGH
When do they rise?

ANNE

Not early – about nine.

CONISBOUGH
Then we will marry at the break of day.
Say six o'clock on Sunday in the chapel
hard by this solar. I know a hedge priest
who'll do the deed and never say a word.
Peter will bring him.

ANNE

Hush! My mother comes!

CONISBOUGH
No matter. When that morning's sun doth shine,
My fortunes will shine too and so will thine.

PETER *(aside)*
Ah'll say this for my lord, 'ee's a fast worker. 'Ee only
met 'er a month ago, an' now 'ee's proposing marriage.
You know, ah could learn summat from 'im. Ah've been
dancin' rahnd Moll fer years, an' got nowheer – but ah
know what to do nah. When I get back to good ol' Coni,
I'll get 'er alone behind t' buttress, whisper that pretty
sonnet into 'er ear, an' ask 'er to marry me.

Exeunt omnes.

SCENE 3

The kitchens at Hereford Castle. TOM and HARRY are talking to MEG and PETER

TOM
T' kitchen at Hereford puts Conisbrough's to shame. Why, ah've never seen so many fat pigs.

HARRY
Them fat pigs is t' garrison men. All they do is eat an' drink and watch t' battle from t' walls.

TOM
If yer keep yer mouth shut, an' yer don't offend 'em, we might do t' same. Ah'd rather ate a fat pig wi' a fat pig than go pig stickin' lean Welshman who are more likely to stick me!

HARRY
If it's stickin' you're talkin' abaht, ah'd rather stick one of them plump chickens over theer.

TOM
So tha prefers fowl dinin' to foul doin'?

HARRY
Aye, but afore I can do fowl dinin' ah've to pluck me chicken first – an' 'ere she is.

Enter MEG.

MEG
Is this what you do in Conisbrough? – Get under our feet in the kitchen when you should be on your feet on the wallwalk?

HARRY
If ah get under yer feet, will yer fall on yer back?

MEG
Not for an oaf like you. I'm waiting for my Prince.

Enter PETER.

TOM
An' 'ere he is, though 'ee's such a skinny youth that if yer was to 'ug 'im yer'd squeeze 'im to death!

MEG
I like a man with a bit more meat on him!

HARRY
What abaht me?

PETER
Enough of yer kitchen rollickings! Ah've just witnessed a real romance, an' ah'll tell yer all abaht it if yer promise to keep it secret.

ALL
We will.

PETER
Yer know that t' Mortimer an' Cherleton families often stay 'ere?

HARRY AND MEG
Aye.

PETER
An' sometimes Mortimer brings 'is daughter, Anne

MEG
A saucy piece of work and not fourteen!

PETER
Well I 'eard talk between the two of them. Me master
said 'ee loved her.

MEG
Loved her? What for? She's just a stick! Why doesn't he
take woman with something to offer?

TOM
She 'a'n't got your ample curves, Meg, but she is a lady.

MEG
Perhaps she is, but I've heard she's penniless.

TOM
Penniless both, then. Gu on Peter. We'll 'ear more.

PETER
It's a gret big secret, an' it would be more than me life's
worth to let it out o' t' bag.

MEG
Nothing's a secret in Hereford Castle until everybody
knows about it!

Enter SERJEANT GOODLAD.

SERJEANT GOODLAD to TOM
Glyndŵr could walk right into Hereford
if it was left to you! Get to your post!
And do it right away or you'll be toast!

Exeunt omnes.

SCENE 4

Outside the chapel near the solar. The priest has gone, and CONISBROUGH and ANNE are having a whispered conversation. PETER is in attendance.

PETER *(aside)*
Ah found t' priest, not in a 'edge, but in a 'ovel that weren't much better. Ah showed 'im t' sovereign me lord 'ad gi'en me, an' it seemed to do t' trick, like. In no time we were in t' private chapel an' they were being pronounced man an' wife. There were nobody else there, so it were up to me to mek me cross on t' parchment as witness to t' ceremony. He's gone nah. 'Urried off to spend 'is sovereign, I reckon, but – what's that I hear? Is someb'dy 'avin' second thoughts?

ANNE
What have we done?

CONISBOUGH
　　　　　　　　　We've turned a little girl
into a woman, and that woman my wife.

ANNE
But we've no money!

CONISBOUGH
　　　　　　　　　I have sworn to rise.
Perhaps my service here will please the king
and he will knight me.

ANNE
　　　　　　　　　I pray that he will.

CONISBOUGH

But there is one more right that I must claim.

ANNE
What right is that?

CONISBOUGH
                My wedding night
when we two will be one.

ANNE
                    What do you mean?

CONISBROUGH
The consummation – that makes it complete.
Without that act a marriage is not marriage
and Holy Church may call it null and void.

ANNE
But what is consummation?

CONISBROUGH
                    A delight
that makes all other ceremonies seem stale.
But it can only take place in my chamber.
Wait till your guardian angels are asleep
and creep up to my solar. Do not fear
my man-at-arms. I've told him not to look.
So do not fail – be there by hook or crook!

Exeunt Omnes.

SCENE V

Outside the solar at Hereford Castle. PETER is waiting outside the door as instructed. We hear the voices of ANNE and CONISBROUGH inside.

PETER *(aside)*
As far as me lord is concerned ah'm invisible, except
when ah really am invisible; what ah mean is – when 'ee
wants summat, an' I ah'm not theer. This time, on 'is
wedding neet, ah were not invisible. Anne saw me, an'
made a bit of a fuss. Said she didna want me watchin'.
Pity! Now I've to wait outside t' door.

Voices within.

CONISBOUGH
Take off your clothes. I want to see you naked.

PETER *(aside)*
Ah did, an' all, so I looked through t' keyoyle. Nah,
keyoyles in 15th century England are big, very big, an' I
'ad a good view, or would 'ave, if t' light 'ad not been
dim, very dim – nowt but a spluttering cresset, in fact.
Well, she were pretty, though ah 'ave to say that Meg's
joke about 'er bein' a stick were true enough.

ANNE
Only my nurse, my mother and duenna...

CONISBOUGH
I am your husband and I have more right
than any other – but I'll teach thee, look!
There goes my doublet, and there goes my shirt!
Off with my codpiece! Next, off with my hose!
There! Man as God designed him in his glory!

ANNE
May heaven help me!

CONISBOUGH
                I'll take you to heaven –

a different one from what you learned in church!
And now it's your turn. Shuffle of that shift
and let me see the ripe fruit underneath.
I'll help you take it off...

PETER *(aside)*
That's Webster tryin' to be poetic – 'ripe fruit' indeed!
'Unripe' 'd be a better word. That bein' said, it were a
dazzlin' sight to a boy who had never seen a woman
starkers, except for that time when t' dairyman's wife
were bathing in t' Don, oh, an' t' time when ah peeked
in t' maid's attic, oh, an'... but yer dunna want to 'ear
abaht me. You want to 'ear more abaht t' love scene in t'
solar. Well, afore ah can tell yer abaht it, I'll 'ave to 'ave
a good look mesen.

The sound of footsteps.

But what's that? The sahnd o' steely sabatons again! It
must be Dick, comin' to report. One last look. Ah! Me
lord 'as 'eard it too, an' has stopped undressin' Anne wi'
'er shift stuck rahnd her head!

CONISBROUGH
                Zounds! What is that knocking?
Begone, I say!

DICK
                My lord, I must report.

CONISBROUGH
Begone!

DICK
                I saw some lights in yonder hills.

CONISBROUGH
Begone! Or I will smack thy pate so hard
thou'll see more lights than at a Yuletide feast!

DICK (to Peter)
Well, thou art witness that ah did me duty.

Exit Dick.

From within.

CONISBROUGH
Now will I teach thee what is meant by love.
The priest said that our love would make us one,
and now I'm going to show you what that means,
for just as we are one in heart and soul
we are about to make two bodies one.

ANNE
But how make one?

CONISBROUGH
                          Did not your mother tell you?

ANNE
She mentioned something about birds and bees.

CONIBROUGH
Then I will show thee. This goes into this,
and then you'll know what's meant by the word 'bliss'.

PETER *(aside)*
That were a scene, ah can tell yer! Better than anythin'
that you lot watches on that Internet thingy. Yer'd like to
see it, ah know, but yer'll never be able to see it from
where you are, e'en through that big keyoyle, so yer can

put yer binoculars away. Ah'd describe it to yer if ah dare, but t' Thought Police 'ave got their eye on Webster an' ah wouldn't want to get 'im into trouble. But since we was speaking o' keyoyles, perhaps a keyoyle metaphor might give yer an idea. Imagine a big key offered up to a small lock. Imagine if that small lock had feelings, 'ow it'd scream an' groan. Funny thing, though, how t' screams an' groans turned into sighs and moans.

Ah couldn't 'elp thinkin' of my Moll. At least after watchin' all that, ah knew what to do, an' ah 'ad the satisfaction o' knowin' that my key would be just the reet size for 'er oyle.

SCENE 6

The Great Hall at Hereford Castle. KING HENRY IV is sitting in state at one end of the hall while CONISBROUGH kneels before him. PETER and several other knights wait to one side.

PETER *(aside)*
It's hard to believe, i'n't it, that a slip o' a girl could put me lord off from 'is great ambition, but she did, an' that's why, a few days later, me lord fahnd himself 'aving to tell a porky pie to the king to try to cover up t' fact that his mind was on a pretty piece of pussycat instead o' Owain Glyndŵr.

KING HENRY IV
You mean to say you never saw him pass?

CONISBOUGH
My man-at-arms saw nothing.

KING HENRY IV

> Bring that man!
Owain Glyndŵr marches before these walls
and you let him pass by! Harry Hotspur
would have sallied forth and overwhelmed him!

Enter DICK.

CONISBOUGH
This is the man, my liege.

KING HENRY IV
> Were you on guard
on Sunday night? If so, what did you see?

DICK
I was, my liege, and saw nothing at all,
except some distant lights that seemed to move.

KING HENRY IV
Did you report this to your lord?

DICK
> I did.

KING HENRY IV
You did your duty well. Now you may go.

Exit DICK.

KING HENRY IV
You did not think to find out what was there?

CONISBOUGH
I took no heed of that report because
you told me I should never sally forth,
but stay within and guard the castle walls

more dearly than I guard my very life.

KING HENRY IV
Methinks that you were careless of your duty,
You should, at least, have sent a scout to look.
Perhaps some revelry distracted you,
or drink had dulled your brain. Perhaps some doxy
got into your bed and made you scout
the hills and valleys of her beauteous body.

RICHARD
Not so, my liege. I followed your commands
to the last letter.

KING HENRY IV
                    That's not good enough!
I want my knights to show initiative.
Ah! Hotspur! Hotspur! Why were you so false?
With you I could have brought Glyndŵr to heel!

Exit KING HENRY IV.

CONISBOUGH
'Tis always thus! I do the best I can.
and this is what I get! I follow orders
and then I'm told I should have broken them.
And if I broke them, it would be the same!
I would be wrong! He cries "Ah! Hotspur! Hotspur!"
but did he not rebel against the king.
Perhaps Hotspur was right and I should take
a leaf out of his book and do the same;
this way, whatever I do, I get the blame!

PETER *(aside)*
Ah do the best ah can, too, an' precious little ah get for
it! When we got back to Coni ah 'ad a go at that little

love scene wi' Moll, but ah got no further than the line: "Marry me, or I will die, I swear!" when she bust out laughin'. "What! Marry a poor page!" she scoffed, "and one who talks like he's never been to school! It's a man-at-arms at least for me. I mean to rise in the world! I don't intend to be a skivvy all my life!

ACT III

PROLOGUE

Enter PETER

Me lord of Conisbrough were lucky, 'cos nob'dy but me 'eard 'is treasonous rant, an' a few years later the king gid him anovver chance to prove 'imself – an' that took us to London. So nah it is 1406 an' yer must imagine that these walls are none other than t' Tower o' London, an' this keep t' White Tower, no less.

SCENE 1

The Great Hall of the White Tower. KING HENRY IV is interviewing bishop FITZ HUGH, Lord SCROPE and CONISBROUGH. PETER is in attendance.

KING HENRY IV
Good bishop Fitz Hugh and my lord of Masham
I bid you welcome, and you, good Conisbrough.
I have a mission which will bring you honour,
and that is to escort my daughter, Philippa,
to Denmark for her marriage to King Eric.

FITZ HUGH
It pleaseth me to serve you as your bishop,
and to assure that everything is done
by Canon Law.

SCROPE
                    You honour me, my liege.
Exeunt FITZ HUGH and SCROPE.

KING HENRY IV
Stay, Conisbrough, I wish to speak with you.
It is not seemly that my daughter's escort
should be a commoner. Only a knight
should be her guard on this her wedding journey.
And thus tomorrow week you will be knighted
with twenty others at Westminster Abbey.
For this I will create you Earl of Cambridge.
Then you will be a lord, and with Lord Scrope
and Lord Fitz Hugh, you'll make an fitting escort:
three lords to laud the daughter of a king!

CONISBROUGH
My liege, I give you deep and heart-felt thanks.

KING HENRY IV
Thank me in the performance of your mission.
You are dismissed.

Exit CONISBROUGH. Outside, he speaks to PETER.

CONISBROUGH
                    Come hither, page, and hear me.
Just as the king with me, I'll make thee higher;
I turn the page and thus pronounce thee, 'squire'.

PETER *(aside)*
So now ah'm a squire – and abaht time, too, for ah'm
nearly 18 years old! No more fetching an' carrying for
me! No more meking up t' fire and laying t' table. Oh
no! I'll be practicing at t' pell wi' Tom, Dick an' 'Arry,
learning to tilt, wi' Dirk to 'elp me into t' saddle, an'

best of all, playin' t' romantic kneet, ah mean, knight, to my Moll! Oh, an' anovver thing. Ah'm goin' to put it on a bit an' start talkin' posh. Nobody ever gets anyweer wi' a Yorkshire accent – at least when it's as broad as mine. Yeah, that's what I'm gunna do. Ah'm gunna talk posh an' learn a bit o' that Norman French – yer know, the real deal, after the school of Stratford-at-Bow.

SCENE 2

On board a ship to Denmark. CAMBRIDGE and SCROPE are talking in a cabin below. PETER has been sent outside, but is listening at the door.

CAMBRIDGE
I left his presence filled with the desire
to serve him loyally, for I felt then
that all my wrongs were righted and that he,
at last, appreciated all my worth.
And then his steward told me that the earldom
came with no grant of land. The Earl of Cambridge
is but a beggar's earldom. What is worse
I have to furnish twenty men-at-arms
from my own pocket to support this mission.
Twenty! I keep but four at Conisbrough these days
the rest are quit-rent men ...

PETER *(aside)*
Every landowner owes military service to his lord, but he can pay a toll instead. That toll is called quit-rent. However, in times of need, a lord can insist on service in person. You should see the quit-rent men of the Honour of Conisbrough! Fat burghers who have never picked up a sword in their lives!

CONISBROUGH

                              They're all I have
but they're unsoldierly to say the least.
They're armed with bits and pieces from my armoury:
rusty old helms, ill-fitting plates armour,
with their pot-bellies hanging out all round.
It makes me feel ashamed to march before them,
a feeling that redoubles what I feel
about the poverty the king has caused.
Why, it seems as though he mocks me with a gift
of knighthood and no money to support it!

SCROPE
I, too, have grievances against the king,
My uncle, Richard Scrope was executed
for playing a part in the Northern Rising.
But soft! A ship is not the pace to speak of this.
These walls of wood are worse than sieves for sound,
and here's the bishop. Ho, Fitz Hugh, what news?

FITZ HUGH
Only that Davy Jones has got my dinner.
He had my breakfast too – I am no sailor.

SCROPE
Well, leave your supper. We will soon be there.

FITZ HUGH
I thank the Lord for that. If I had known
I would have stayed in London on my own.

SCENE 3

*Outside Lund Cathedral. PETER describes the wedding
ceremony.*

PETER

I sometimes wonder if Webster has heard of the classical unities of time, place and action, because this play is all over the place! He'd say that Shakespeare's *Henry V* is just as bad, and I suppose he'd be right. Anyway, now you must imagine that these stone walls are the walls of Lund Cathedral – and that shouldn't be too difficult because it was built in 1080 and has the same stark, Romanesque style as this castle.

It was a wonderful wedding, though I couldn't help feeling sorry for the poor girl, who was only 12. Funny, isn't it? There she was, a daughter of the king of England, and she had no say whatever in the business. My Moll, on the other hand, though only a kitchen maid, has a very big say – too much, if you ask me!

I know you'd like me to describe the wedding, but I'm not very good at that sort of thing. I can tell you that they followed the Danish custom of coming through a Gate of Honour – a fine archway of evergreen foliage and flowers which had been set up outside the west portal, and that she wore a tunic with a cloak in white silk bordered with grey squirrel and ermine, and that poor Philippa looked as though she was about to cry when the priest said the words, "Jeg nu udtale dig mand og kone" which is Danish for, "I now pronounce thee man and wife."

As PETER is speaking a dumb show is played out behind him showing the wedding ceremony.

SCENE 4

The wedding reception at the Merchant Taylor's Hall, Lund. We can only see one of the lower tables at which SERJEANT GOODLAD, TOM, DICK, HARRY, PETER and two DANISH MEN-AT-ARMS are sitting.

PETER *(aside)*
Now we're in the Merchant Taylor's Hall for the wedding reception. For once, I am not in attendance on my lord Cambridge. There are far grander servants than me to do that today.

TOM
'Fore God, they have given me a rouse already.

DICK
Good faith, a little one; not past a pint, as I am a soldier.

HANS
Bringe øl, ho!

Sings.

And let me the canakin clink, clink;
And let me the canakin clink
A soldier's a man;
A life's but a span;
Why, then, let a soldier drink.
Some wine, boys!

LEIF
'Fore God, an excellent song.

HANS
I learned it in England, where, indeed, they are most potent in potting: your Dane, your German, and your swag-bellied Hollander – drikke, ho! – are nothing
to your English.

LEIF

Is your Englishman so expert in his drinking?

HANS
Why, he drinks you, with facility, your Dane dead drunk; he sweats not to overthrow your Almain; he gives your Hollander a vomit, ere the next pottle can be filled.

LEIF
Well, we'll see about that. Bringe øl, ho!

TOM
It ain't fair!

DICK
Why?

TOM
Because their so-called beer'll blow me up before it knocks me dahn!

LEIF
I've tried your so-called beer – it's flat.

DICK
It's t' best beer in t' world as ah'll prove if yer'll stand up like a man.

SERJEANT GOODLAD
Now, boys, let's not spoil a good booze up! Here's to the English and the Danish who have the best beer in the world, and can outdrink everybody!

ALL
Aye! Ja!

PETER *(aside)*

I seem to have heard those words before – is Webster plagiarising again? Well, if he is, at least there'll be one part of the play that will be worth hearing! Anyway, what I really wanted to say was that the only one who doesn't seem to be enjoying himself is my master. Oh, he's putting a brave face on it with a forced grin that would turn wine sour, but I can see that he's seething with resentment. I only hope that little chat I overheard on the ship doesn't come to anything.

ACT IV

PROLOGUE

Enter PETER.

PETER
The years fly by, don't they? It is now 1411 and I am 23. I'm still a squire, though by rights I should now be a man-at-arms on a penny a day – never mind, being a squire was enough to get Moll. We're betrothed, and trying to scrape together enough money to set up a little public house which I've a mind to call *The Eagle*. But you don't want to hear about me. You came here to watch a play about Richard of Conisbrough, so let's get on with it.

My lord's fortunes picked up a little when his daughter, Isabel, was born. Soon after that, his marriage was recognised by the Pope and the king awarded his wife an annuity of £50 – not that it did much to improve matters at Conisbrough. The roof of the great hall still leaked, and the timbers of the drawbridge were so rotten that we dared not pull it up. It was this desperate poverty that gave my lord the idea of selling his daughter – I exaggerate, of course. He did not literally sell her, but tried to get money through an arranged marriage.

SCENE 1

Conisbrough Castle, the Great Chamber. CAMBRIDGE

*is in discussion with GREY over an arranged marriage
between his daughter Isabel and Grey's son, Thomas.
ANNE, who is heavily pregnant, is not happy about the
idea. Little Isabel can be seen in the background playing
with her nurse, while young Thomas Grey looks at her
doubtfully. PETER is in attendance.*

ANNE
Isabel is but a babe! She's only three!

CAMBRIDGE
Early betrothal is quite common now.
I heard that Spain's Infanta was betrothed
at nine years old.

ANNE
                    Nine, that is well – but three!
Am I to sell my children one by one?
Is this one in my womb to be the next?

CAMBRIDGE
We can delay the marriage for a while.

ANNE
For a long while, and in that time who knows
what changes may occur in our estate –
or yours, Sir Thomas, for – may I be frank?

GREY
In weighty matters it is always best.

ANNE
I've heard that you are not much better off
than we are. That your lands are all entailed.

GREY

Then you heard wrong. 'Tis true the revenues
from my estates are less than I would like,
but I, ever the solider, since I came of age,
am in the service of Prince of Wales,
and he, as you'd expect a royal prince
rewards me royally.

CAMBRIDGE
                              I'm glad of that
For I can give no dowry but the lordship
of Wark-in-Tyndale at a bargain price.

GREY
You give me land and then ask me to pay?

CAMBRIDGE
I would that I could give it you outright,
but you know well enough my empty pockets.
The land is good, though pays poor revenues
because I lack the funds wherewith to clear it.
Pay me the price, then clear the land yourself,
and you will have such revenues from the land
your outlay will be covered in a year.

GREY
I'll be frank too. Your 'gift' is just a 'sale' –
and at a steep price too! What do you think? –
That I am green and to be gulled so easily!
What? Pay you for the lordship, and then pay
to clear the land, and then pay to hire workers!
I would be out of pocket till I die!

CAMBRIDGE
Not so! The land is good! You'll make a fortune!

GREY

Then why...

CAMBRIDGE
                    I have no money in my purse
for coals or candles – as for clearing land!

GREY
I understand, and I'll accept your offer,
but not because I think it is a good one.
The truth is, you have something else I want.

CAMBRIDGE
Which is?

GREY
                   Royal connections for my son.
That royal coat of arms you wear so lightly:
arms of the kingdom, differenced by a label
argent of three points, explains it all.
You may be poor, but you are part and parcel
of those blood ties that form the royal lineage.

CAMBRIDGE
And what good has it done me?

GREY
                             Well, not much,
but my son Thomas may well reap the benefit.

ANNE
My lord, a word alone.

GREY
                  Excuse me, Grey.

ANNE

For the last time, I beg you, think again.
Thomas is 12. Soon he will be a man
with man's desires. Isabel is three,
and by the time she's old enough for marriage
he will be twenty-four or twenty-five.

CAMBRIDGE
Then he will have to find a willing wench
and tumble her, or pay a harlot's price.

ANNE
I know that's what men do, but hear my words:
if he should try to take my Isabel
before her blood has come, and she a woman
then I will rend him like a lioness
fighting in protection of her cubs.

CAMBRIDGE
I'll second you in that, and that being so,
are we agreed?

ANNE
                    Aye, with a heavy heart.

PETER *(aside)*
And that is how my lord came to be acquainted with
Lord Grey. He had thought to dupe him and fill his
purse, but Lord Grey was not as wealthy as he had
boasted, and couldn't find the price of the lordship of
Wark-in-Tyndale. Thus, Cambridge continued as poor as
ever.

SCENE 2

*The Great Hall at Conisbrough Castle. CAMBRIDGE is
celebrating the birth of his son, Richard. He is attended*

by PETER, but we can't see them. We see only the lower table with SERJEANT GOODLAD, TOM, DICK and HARRY.

TOM
Why, ah've not seen such revelry as this since we were in Denmark.

DICK
Nor I, ever at Conisbrough.

HARRY
Well, 'tis the old Conisbrough custom called 'wettin' t'bairn's 'ead'. It's good to see one o' these trumped up Norman lords followin' t' old customs.

TOM
Norman? 'Ees as English as you are!

DICK
Ah'm Welsh. Well me dad was.

TOM
We're all mixed up now, anyway.

DICK
Mixed up or not. 'Is lot is till on top.

HARRY
On top! 'Ee's got no money. 'Ee must have visited t' Jews.

TOM
Well, ah dunna care weer 'ee gorrit from, ah'm goin' to wet me whistle good an' proper.

Enter SERJEANT GOODLAD

SERJEANT GOODLAD
No you're not. You're on guard. Go to the gatehouse.

DICK
Dunna worry, Tom. We'll save yer a pottle!

SERJEANT GOODLAD
And you're on your usual beat – on top of the keep!

HARRY
Ah suppose ah'm on duty as well. Weer shall I go?

SERJEANT GOODLAD
Here, with me – I need somebody to share my revels!

TOM
Harry 'as all t' luck!

DICK
T' biggest feast e'er seen in Coni, an' ah miss it!

SERJEANT GOODLAD
Don't fret. The quit-rent men will be here soon. They'll
relieve you.

TOM
If they turn aht at all.

DICK
If they dunna, ah'll gu an' drag 'em aht!

CAMBRIDGE
Lordynges, commoners, burghers and all,
I welcome you to share this happy day.

A son is born to us – we called him Richard,
and he will be the Duke of York one day.
No greater joy is known to us than this,
for in a son we are reborn again,
for in a son our name is carried on,
and in a son is immortality,
at least the only kind that man can know.
His birth has fired anew my old ambition,
to rise in wealth and honour. Thus, I vow
before you all that I will win for him
the lands and revenues that I am owed.
Now fill your pots and raise a toast with me
To Richard, Duke of York – third of that name!
May he, like me, win favour, friends and fame!

ALL
To Richard, Duke of York!

SCENE 3

Outside the solar at Conisbrough Castle. The PRIEST and the Conisbrough LEECH are breaking some bad news to CAMBRIDGE. PETER is in attendance.

PETER *(aside)*
In Conisbrough Church there is a stained glass window – and before you go looking for it, I am sorry to say that it was smashed by a Puritan and is no longer there. It shows a picture of a popular medieval image: the Wheel of Fortune. The rich and happy are at the top, the poor and unfortunate are at the bottom. The thing is, of course, that the wheel keeps turning, and I am sorry to say, that it turned for my lord Cambridge. At the feast of the Wetting of the Baby's Head, Cambridge was at the top, but here we are, only a few days after, and it looks as though he's right at the bottom again.

LEECH
My lord, it was the dreaded childbed fever.
I did my best. I bled her like horse,
made her inhale hot fumes of Mercury
and drink a potion made of Belladonna.
But all to no avail. She writhed and screamed
then, weakening, she breathed her last and died.

PRIEST
But not before I gave her Final Unction
so now her soul is on its way to Heaven
Be comforted in that.

CAMBRIDGE
                         How speak of comfort?
My only love, my dearest Anne, is gone;
my best friend, comforter in all my trials,
support in sorrow, sharer of my joys,
mother of my children – how can I go on!

PRIEST
Be comforted – Our Lord succours our grief.
He died upon the cross for us, remember.
Then rose again, teaching us not to fear
Death, whatever dreadful form it takes.

CAMBRIDGE
I thank thee for thy spiritual counsel,
and thee, good Leech, I thank thee for thy skill.
Now leave me on my own to dwell upon
the question that is thrust upon my life –
how can I live without her?

PRIEST
                         But alone?
It is not good to brood alone with grief.

CAMBRIDGE
I have my squire to tend to any needs.

PRIEST
Well, then, may God be with you in your loss.

Exeunt PRIEST and LEECH.

CAMBRIDGE
What is this cocktail burning in my breast?
Somehow my grief is boiling into rage,
making me rail against the universe –
now, I defy you – Stars! And you, King Henry!
For now I plan to rise by any means –
whether they're foul or fair, it matters not.
What, fair! Have I not tried throughout the years?
Defended Hereford against Glyndŵr,
Escorted Princess Philippa abroad –
and what have I to show for it – a knighthood
that's meaningless without grant of land;
a miserable £50 annuity,
and that not mine, but granted to my wife,
which now will stop. Fair means are foul
and foul are fair, and now will aid my purpose.
And I have other aid – I'm not alone.
Lord Scrope, I know, has reasons to rebel,
and Thomas Grey is just as poor as I.
I'll sound them out – but what shall be our cause?
Edmund de Mortimer's right to be king!
He was the heir presumptive to King Richard,
and is supported by some English nobles,
and Grey among them – why, he is his kinsman!
And when King Edmund sits upon the throne,
he will reward the men who put him there.
The highest honours, caracutes of land,
titles and privileges beyond count

the grateful king will heap upon our heads.
That settled, I'll sound out Lord Scrope and Grey.
and with their help I'll see a brighter day!

PETER *(aside)*
That was the straw that broke the camel's back. Look, Richard is a Conisbrough man, born and bred, so he can't be that bad, can he? He tried, he really did. He endured more than most men could endure, but when Fate poleaxed him with the death of his beloved Anne, I believe he went mad. So when we go into the final act, don't think too badly of him, will you?

ACT V

PROLOGUE

Enter PETER

PETER
It took a few years to hatch the conspiracy, with the result that, by the time it was ready, King Henry IV had died and in 1413, King Henry V became king of England. I'm sure that my lord Cambridge, would rather have had his revenge on King Henry IV, but Fortune's Wheel was turning too fast for him. He revised his plans, and saw his opportunity when, on 19th April 1415, the Great Council agreed to Henry's request to sanction war with France. Southampton, the embarkation point for Henry V's army, was to be the place where the conspiracy would at last be carried to a conclusion.

So, you must now imagine that these walls are the walls of the Red Lion Inn in Southampton where the last remaining details of the conspiracy were plotted.

SCENE 1

The tap room in the Red Lion Inn in Southampton. TOM, DICK, HARRY and SERJEANT GOODLAD are discussing the French campaign.

TOM
Ah've never seen so many men-at-arms!

DICK
It meks yer proud to be English!

HARRY
But not to be from Conisbrough. Our lot's a disgrace.

TOM
Beggin' yer pardon, this is my best surcoat.

HARRY
No, not us. Them quit-rent men. I 'eard that King Henry called for a 'undred from Coni – but it's twenty like it allus is, and most o' 'em look like they've been kitted aht in a junkyard!

TOM
Well, there's four o' us. Five if yer count Peter. Then t' quit-rent men, an' me lord 'ad to leave a few to guard t' castle.

DICK
Why? Who'd want that? It's fallin' dahn. I'll tell yer, ah'm none too 'appy when ah'm on duty on t' south curtain – wobbly it is!

SERJEANT GOODLAD
Come on lads! One more drink and to bed with you. We're off tomorrow morning to fight the French!

TOM
Why?

DICK
'Aven't you 'eard? It's the 'undred years war.

HARRY

What? Ah thought that 'ad finished.

TOM
It 'ad, but King Henry started it again.

DICK
Why?

HARRY
Dunno. I'm more worried about what they's plottin'
upstairs.

SERJEANT GOODLAD
Yours is not to wonder why, lad, yours is to do and die
with a Frog crossbow bolt through your thick skull. Now
drink up, and get to bed!

SCENE 2

*An upper room in the Red Lion Inn in Southampton.
CAMBRIDGE, SCROPE and GREY are plotting.
MORTIMER is with them. PETER is in the room at first,
but is sent outside.*

CAMBRIDGE
Peter, wait you outside and guard the door.
Let no man enter here on pain of death.

MORTIMER
It might be best to send your man downstairs.

CAMBRIDGE
Not so, for Peter never, ever tells a secret.

Exit PETER.

And now, my lords, let's put the final gloss
upon the plan that has waited so long.

GREY
King Henry's sudden whim gives us our chance.
In the confusion of the embarkation
he'll find a sudden dagger in his ribs.

SCROPE
But how? My lords, it will not be so easy.
I am his right-hand man and know him well –
so well that I have shared his bed and board,
been privy to his counsel, and enjoyed
privileges that most can only dream of.

GREY
Then why...?

SCROPE
Cambridge has heard it, and I thought you knew
how my poor uncle, Richard Scrope was treated.
But to take up my point – I know him well,
and know how vigilantly he is guarded.
A hundred men-at-arms attend him daily,
and he goes nowhere – no, not ev'n the privy
without a man-at-arms on either side.

GREY
I have heard something of it. We're in luck
to have among us one close to the king.

CAMBRIDGE
Indeed, and that will be essential to my plan:
With the next tide, King Henry will set sail,
and all Scrope's men will be upon his ship.
The gangplank he must cross is one foot wide

and can only take one man at a time.
And we'll be on the ship to welcome him,
though not with bows and scrapes – rather with this!

He produces a dagger.

Ha! I see you blanching at the thought,
but I, who've suffered most from royal disfavour,
will play a Casca, and will strike him first.
Then you, Lord Grey, must strike second blow.
Scrope, you'll be last, playing the part of Brutus.
and when he cries, "Et tu, Masham?" say, "Aye,
'tis my revenge for Richard's execution!"
Then will your waiting soldiers draw their arms,
and dare the bodyguard to cross the gangpank.
At the same time, good Mortimer, will you
step forward to the view of all the people
and stand beside Lord Scrope, and I will shout:
"King Henry, the usurper, now lies dead!
And so long live the rightful king, King Edmund!"
Then I will make a speech like Brutus made
to justify the end he made of Caesar:

He takes out a paper and reads from it.

Englishmen, countrymen, and friends! hear me for my
cause, and be silent, that you may hear. As Henry
honoured me, I weep for him; as he was fortunate, I
rejoice at it; as he was valiant, I honour him: but, as he
was ambitious, I slew him. Yes, countrymen. He was
ambitious. He would have dragged us into a ruinous war
with France which would have reduced the country to
penury. He is not even the legitimate king. You see
before you King Edmund – a direct descendant of
Edward the Confessor. Who is here so vile that will not
love his country? If any, speak; for him have I offended.

I pause for a reply...

SCROPE
It is a fine, speech, Cambridge. But 'tis all to do
before you can deliver it. Now, your plan...

GREY
The plan is good. Can you think of a better?

SCROPE
What think you Mortimer, is the plan good?

MORTIMER
I had not thought that you... What I mean is...

SCROPE
Come, Edmund, this is your great chance,
and it is we, not you, who wield the knife!

MORTIMER
Then I agree.

SCROPE
     Well then, we are adjourned.

CAMBRIDGE
Not yet. There's one more thing. Edmund must sign.
For I have suffered from kings' empty promises.
I have prepared these papers for this meeting,
copies for all of us. They grant us land
and titles, so that we will reap the benefit
of that great deed that we must do tomorrow.
Come now, sign all!

GREY
     In writing is much danger.

CAMBRIDGE

In empty promises there's more – come, sign!

SCROPE

A word would hang us, so what is the difference?
I'll sign the papers.

GREY

                        Then I'll sign them too.

CAMBRIDGE

Here's yours, my lord, and yours, and yours
Lord Edmund – no, I should say king.

MORTIMER

                                    Adieu,
until tomorrow when we'll see this through.

Exeunt all except PETER.

PETER

I tried not to listen, I really did, but even with both
fingers in my ears I could not block out those treasonous
plans! And now that I have heard it, what am I to do? I
love and honour my lord Cambridge, even though he
should have made me a man-at-arms years ago. I don't
blame him for that. I know he has no money. I also know
that his heart's in the right place and that he has had a lot
to suffer at the hand of kings – but this! I am a loyal
Englishman above everything else – so am I to run to the
king and tell all? If I did, wouldn't that be a kind of
treason against my master? Oh, I am in horrible dilemma
– and don't know what to do about it!

SCENE 3

Enter PETER.

PETER

I was pacing up and down all night trying to decide where my loyalties lay – were they with Conisbrough and my lord, or with England and the king? Eventually I fell asleep and had a bad dream. In my dream I saw the Saxon king, King Edward the Confessor, and he was pointing at Edmund Mortimer and saying, "Behold my lineage!". That was my answer – I was a Saxon, and my lord was a descendant of a Norman conqueror – or was he? Hadn't our peoples got all mixed up since those distant days? I was awoken by the sound of heavy boots, but heavy boots or not, I still didn't know what to do.

The boots were the boots of King Henry's guard, and they had come to summon my master, Scrope and Grey into the Royal Presence. It was worrying that they should be sent for in this way, but perhaps it was the urgency of the situation, the fleet being likely to put to sea any day now. There was no sign of Mortimer who, it seemed, had left the inn in the middle of the night. I followed them to Southampton Castle and into the Great Hall, where King Henry was waiting.

I should warn you, by the way, that the next scene is almost wholly a rip-off of Shakespeare's *Henry V*. Well, for once, I don't blame Webster. He has already plagiarised bits of *Romeo and Juliet*, *Othello* and *Julius Caesar* and it would have been crazy to stop short now, for this is the moment when – no, I can't tell you, it would be a story spoiler. Only those of you who paid attention in History lessons will know what happened. What? You didn't study British history? Shame on somebody! But this is no time for a diatribe against Political Correctness. Let's find out what happened to the conspirators.

SCENE 4

The Great Hall of Southampton Castle. KING HENRY V is holding an audience with CAMBRIDGE, SCROPE and GREY. Many guards and nobleman, including EXETER, are present. PETER is peering through the door.

KING HENRY V
Now sits the wind fair, and we will aboard.
My Lord of Cambridge, and my kind Lord of Masham,
and you, my gentle knight, give me your thoughts:
think you not that the powers we bear with us
will cut their passage through the force of France,
doing the execution and the act
for which we have in head assembled them?

SCROPE
No doubt, my liege, if each man do his best.

KING HENRY V
I doubt not that; since we are well persuaded
we carry not a heart with us from hence
that grows not in a fair consent with ours,
nor leave not one behind that doth not wish
success and conquest to attend on us.

CAMBRIDGE
Never was monarch better feared and loved
than is your majesty: there's not, I think, a subject
that sits in heart-grief and uneasiness
under the sweet shade of your government.

GREY

True: those that were your father's enemies
have steeped their galls in honey and do serve you
with hearts create of duty and of zeal.

KING HENRY V
We therefore have great cause of thankfulness;
and shall forget the office of our hand,
sooner than quittance of desert and merit
according to the weight and worthiness.

SCROPE
So service shall with steeled sinews toil,
and labour shall refresh itself with hope,
to do your grace incessant services.

KING HENRY V
And now to our French causes:
who are the late commissioners?

CAMBRIDGE
I one, my lord:
your highness bade me ask for it to-day.

SCROPE
So did you me, my liege.

GREY
And I, my royal sovereign.

KING HENRY V
Then, Richard Earl of Cambridge, there is yours;
there yours, Lord Scrope of Masham; and, sir knight,
Grey of Northumberland, this same is yours:
read them; and know, I know your worthiness.
My Lord of Westmoreland, and uncle Exeter,
we will aboard to night. Why, how now, gentlemen!

What see you in those papers that you lose
so much complexion? Look ye, how they change!
their cheeks are paper. Why, what read you there
that hath so cowarded and chased your blood
out of appearance?

CAMBRIDGE
I do confess my fault;
and do submit me to your highness' mercy.

GREY SCROPE
To which we all appeal.

KING HENRY V
You must not dare, for shame, to talk of mercy;
for your own reasons turn into your bosoms,
as dogs upon their masters, worrying you.
See you, my princes, and my noble peers,
these English monsters! My Lord of Cambridge here,
you know how apt our love was to accord
to furnish him with all appertinents
belonging to his honour; But, O,
what shall I say to thee, Lord Scrope? thou cruel,
ingrateful, savage and inhuman creature!
Thou that didst bear the key of all my counsels,
that knew'st the very bottom of my soul,
that almost mightst have coined me into gold.
For this revolt of thine, methinks, is like
another fall of man. Their faults are open:
arrest them to the answer of the law;
and God acquit them of their practises!

EXETER
I arrest thee of high treason, by the name of
Richard Earl of Cambridge.
I arrest thee of high treason, by the name of

Henry Lord Scrope of Masham.
I arrest thee of high treason, by the name of
Thomas Grey, knight, of Northumberland.

KING HENRY V
God quit you in his mercy! Hear your sentence.
Touching our person seek we no revenge;
but we our kingdom's safety must so tender,
whose ruin you have sought, that to her laws
we do deliver you. Get you therefore hence,
poor miserable wretches, to your death:
the taste whereof, God of his mercy give
you patience to endure, and true repentance
of all your dear offences! Bear them hence.

Exeunt CAMBRIDGE, SCROPE and GREY, guarded.

PETER *(aside)*
How was my lord betrayed? Did I, perhaps, sleepwalk to
the king and tell him all? Or... no, Edmund Mortimer is
the betrayer, I feel sure. I could tell that his heart wasn't
in it while I was listening, and he went somewhere in the
middle of the night – to tell all to the king, perhaps. Yes,
it must be he, or he would have been condemned with
the others just now.

SCENE 5

*A dungeon in Southampton Castle. CAMBRIDGE is in a
cell, alone.*

CAMBRIDGE
I have been studying how I may compare
this prison where I live unto the world:
and for because the world is populous
and here is not a creature but myself,

I cannot do it; so my mind returns
to those sweet scenes of childhood in Conisbrough,
fishing in the brook near to the mill,
or swimming in the River Don in summer.
Ah! how we laughed, unknowing of the cares
that would come with adulthood. Then my mind
wanders to those endearing scenes of courtship.
I'm back in Hereford again with Anne
and she is in my arms, and we, in heaven.
And then, the prattling of our little Isabel,
and the birth of my son for whom I wished
so much – too much indeed! And then – her death...
But no, I will not think on that. It was too much
for my poor heart to bear and drove me mad
and now I feel that madness ebbing from me.
I see now that I should have lived my life
while it was happening, and not wasted it
in wishing for what could not be. Ah well!
I have one night to live it all again
in my imagination.

He hears a sound.

Who is that?

PETER
'Tis I, Peter, your squire. What can I bring you?

CAMBRIDGE
A pardon would be best, but failing that
bring me a pint of wine!

PETER goes out for a moment to get the wine.

PETER

Here 'tis, my lord.

CAMBRIDGE
Peter, you have served me a long and loyally,
borne my neglect and yet kept all my counsel –
Nay, have no fear, I know it was not you
who played the tittle-tattle to the king.
'Twas Edmund, may God curse him for a traitor!
And yet – that's me – how came I to this pass?
Bring me a priest, I must confess myself.
But soft! Before you go, a final word.
Take this – my seal. 'Tis made of solid gold
and it will furnish thee for my neglect.
Marry thy Moll and sometimes think of me.
Open that inn thou often tolds't me of,
and when thou art an innkeeper and free
raise thou a tankard in my memory.

PETER *(aside)*
I don't often cry, but that speech – and his generous gift
– cracked me up, I can tell you. See, I told you that he
wasn't all bad. We all do stupid things from time to
time, but my lord had to pay for his stupidity with his
head.

SCENE 6

Outside Bargate, Southampton, where a platform and a
chopping block have been set up for the execution of the
traitors. KING HENRY V and his nobles, including
EXETER, look on. PETER is on the edges of the crowd.

CAMBRIDGE
I do repent me of my treachery
and humbly beg your highness' pardon.
It was a kind of madness brought upon me
by cruel fate and your forbears' neglect –
though I have no intent to make complaint

and do accept the judgement passed upon me.
I see now that the hand of cruel Fate
smites everybody without fear or favour,
from humble peasant to the highest king.
And as for being passed over, many a man
lacks the promotion that his skill deserves,
while those who, like sheep in the nursery rhyme,
reply with "Yes, sir, yes, sir. Three bags full,"
are showered with riches. 'Tis the common lot
to lose a loved one to the feared Grim Reaper.
So I was wrong to take these things to heart
and stir up a rebellion 'gainst the king.
And now I place my head upon the block,
as a just punishment for my misdeeds.

He gives gold to the executioner.

This is for thee, make sure the axe falls true!
For my whole life led to this noble thing:
an execution fitted for a king!

Kneels to the block. The axe falls.

EXETER
Nothing in his life became him like the leaving it.

EPILOGUE

Enter PETER.

PETER
If I did not admire my lord so much I would call him a
fool because I lived long enough to see that he had
thrown away his life for nothing. With the death of the
Duke of York, my lord's elder brother, at the Battle of
Agincourt later that year, his son, Richard Plantagenet

became heir to the title. Richard had twelve children, one of whom became, King Richard III – what more could my master have aspired to?

By the way, I used my master's generous gift to open my public house, and I called it *The Eagle* as I had intended – though with an addition. Moll had just given birth to our daughter, so in honour of that event, I called my inn *The Eagle and Child*, and if you're ever passing that way, drop in, and we'll share a pint while reflecting on the good old days when Richard of Conisbrough was lord of Conisbrough Castle.

HISTORICAL NOTE

Richard of Conisbrough was born in Conisbrough Castle only a few hundred yards from my family home in Castle Avenue, and of all the great noblemen who owned Conisbrough Castle, he was the one who spent most time there. I have referred to him as 'Richard' in this article, though in the play he is referred to by his titles, according to the contemporary practice.

Richard was born in 1375, the second son of Edmund of Langley, 1st Duke of York, and his first wife, Isabella of Castille. His godfather was King Richard II. Richard was two years younger than his brother, Edward. Richard received no lands from his father, perhaps because Langley did not recognize him as a legitimate child. G. L. Harriss (2004) has suggested that he may have been the child of an illicit liaison between his mother and John Holland, 1st Duke of Exeter, and this is the interpretation that I have taken in my play, the discontented "bastard" being a common character in Elizabethan drama.

Richard's mother, on the other hand, did make an attempt to provide for him. She named King Richard II as her heir before her death on 23 December 1392 and requested him to grant her younger son an annuity of 500 marks. The king complied. On 3 February 1393, he provided his godson with an annuity of £100 from the revenues in Yorkshire that Isabella had formerly received, and on 16 March 1393, he provided him with a further annuity of £233 6s 8d from the Exchequer. However, Richard II was deposed in 1399 and Richard of Conisbrough seemed to be out of favour with the new king, Henry IV, and his annuities ceased to paid. The arrangement that his mother made in her will effectively meant that Richard did not even own the revenues of the Honour of Conisbrough, and the resulting poverty was undoubtedly the major cause of his discontent. I chose to start my play at this point, with Richard reacting to a letter in which the king stated that he refused to make any further payments.

From April 1403 to October 1404, Richard commanded a small force defending Herefordshire against the Welsh rebel leader Owain Glyndŵr, but never had an opportunity to show his mettle. It was at this time that he met his future wife Anne de Mortimer, which gave me an opportunity to make up a little love scene (and plagiarise a few lines from *Romeo and Juliet*, as well as borrowing a motif from the bard's most famous sonnet).

In 1406, together with the Bishop of Bath, Lord Fitz Hugh, and Lord Scrope, he was chosen to escort King Henry's daughter Philippa to Denmark for her marriage to King Eric (Danish Erik af Pommern, c. 1381 – c. 1459). Richard was knighted in July of that year, probably to make him more suitable as an escort for the king's daughter. To keep things simple, I conflated this event with his creation as third Earl of Cambridge, which actually took place in 1414.

His daughter, Isabel, was born in 1409, and his son, Richard of York, in 1411. His wife died soon after. Once again, to keep an already over-complex narrative simple, I omitted all mention of his second wife, Maud Clifford, the divorced wife of John Neville, 6th Baron Latimer. I made the death of his first wife, Anne, a turning point in my play, after which he pursues the idea of rebellion with a kind of madness, and begins to put together what became known as the Southampton Plot. Richard conspired with Lord Scrope and Sir Thomas Grey to depose King Henry and place his late wife Anne's brother Edmund Mortimer, 5th Earl of March, on the throne. On 31 July, Mortimer revealed the plot to the king. The conspirators were condemned to death and 5 August 1415, six days before the fleet set sail to France.

Shakespeare attributed the Southampton Plot to the machinations of the French who devised it to balk the forthcoming invasion. However, most modern historians disagree, so I omitted that interpretation of events.

I will admit to exercising considerable poetic licence in my treatment of Richard. He was a Conisbrough lad, after all, and as a fellow Conisbrough lad, I cannot be too hard on him. Accordingly, I have had him 'see the light' while reflecting in prison, and then portrayed him facing his executioners with a noble speech – an attempted Aristotelian development beginning with *Hamartia* (a fatal flaw, in this case, ambition), leading to *Anagnorisis* (a realisation of the truth of matters) and ending with *Catharsis* (a powerful release of healing emotions). Well, that was the idea, I'm not the Swan of Avon, as Peter pointed out in his prologue, I am better described as the Crow of Conisbrough, but I hope I managed to get at least a shadow of the Aristotelian stuff in there!

My historical research was based on various Internet sources, including Wikipedia, but principally on an excellent book entitled *Henry V and the Southampton Plot* of 1415 by T.B. Pugh, 1988.

ABOUT THE AUTHOR

Christopher Webster was brought up in Conisbrough, went to Station Road School, and has lived at various times on Daylands Avenue, Roberts Avenue and Castle Avenue. The town, with its rich history, has been an important influence in his life, and has inspired some of his best work. He read English at St David's, Lampeter, and Leeds University, and has taught English in several countries, including Germany, Bermuda, Belgium and Singapore. His first educational publication was *Poetry Through Humour and Horror* (Cassell, 1987). This was followed by many more, including books for KS3 and GCSE English Language and Literature published by Hodder. He has also written several novels, including novels about Conisbrough history, most recently, *The Abduction of Lady Alice*, and a collection of narrative poems called *Conisbrough Tales*, which he describes as "a *Canturbury Tales* for Conisbrough".